LILY
TO THE rescue

THE
NOT-SO-STINKY
SKUNK

ALSO BY W. BRUCE CAMERON

W. BRUCE CAMERON

LILY
TO THE rescue

THE NOT-SO-STINKY SKUNK

Illustrations by
JENNIFER L. MEYER

A TOM DOHERTY ASSOCIATES BOOK

NEW YORK

LILY TO THE RESCUE: THE NOT-SO-STINKY SKUNK

Copyright © 2020 by W. Bruce Cameron
Illustrations © 2020 by Jennifer L. Meyer

A Starscape Book
Published by Tom Doherty Associates
120 Broadway
New York, NY 10271

www.tor-forge.com

The Library of Congress Cataloging-in-Publication Data
is available upon request.

ISBN 978-1-250-23448-3 (trade paperback)
ISBN 978-1-250-23447-6 (hardcover)
ISBN 978-1-250-23446-9 (ebook)

Our books may be purchased in bulk for promotional, educational, or business use. Please contact your local bookseller or the Macmillan Corporate and Premium Sales Department at 1-800-221-7945, extension 5442, or by email at MacmillanSpecialMarkets@macmillan.com.

First Edition: September 2020

Printed in the United States of America

0 9 8 7 6 5 4 3 2

Dedicated to Georgia Lee Cameron and all the other wonderful people saving lives at Life is Better Rescue in Denver, Colorado. I am very proud of all the work you do!

LILY

TO THE rescue

THE NOT-SO-STINKY SKUNK

1

"Lily, Lily, Lily!" Maggie Rose said to me. "We're going camping, Lily!"

Maggie Rose is my girl, and I am her dog. When she is happy, I am *very* happy. When she is excited, I am *very* excited. She was obviously excited and happy at this moment, so I jumped up to put my feet on her knees and then dropped down to run in circles around the kitchen. Whatever was going on, it was the best!

I looked up, wagging, when Mom came in the kitchen carrying a bag. I could smell something delicious in that bag!

"We were out of dog food, so I brought some from the shelter," Mom said. She set the bag down and I padded over to sniff it more carefully. "Would you put it in the pantry, Maggie Rose?"

I was excited when Maggie Rose lifted the bag, grunting a little. "Can you get it?" Mom asked. "It's heavy."

"I got it," my girl replied. I followed her, my nose up, as she put the bag in a closet and shut the door. She skipped back into the kitchen, though I felt that a celebration could include opening the bag at that moment.

"You are such a help with all the animals, Maggie Rose," Mom said, praising her. "I really appreciate everything you do for our rescue operation."

"And Lily!" my girl replied. "Don't forget, she's a rescue, too!"

"And Lily," Mom agreed.

My girl and I ran into the living room, where the floor is softer. We had a very good wrestle with an old towel because we were both so happy.

"Dad's taking us, Lily," Maggie Rose whis-

pered. "We're going up to the mountains. I *never* get to spend time with just Dad!"

I love it when my girl talks to me. I jumped into her lap and licked her ear and under her chin, where she tastes especially delicious.

I didn't know what she was telling me, but I knew it was good.

Maggie Rose flopped down on her back so that I could lie down on top of her and pant in her face.

"Dad says we're going to take care of some prairie dogs first," she told me. I heard the word "dogs" and licked her chin again. Obviously, whatever she was talking about was going to be very good, because she'd said "dogs."

"And then we'll go and camp. You and me and Dad." Maggie Rose hugged me. "Just us!"

"Hey," said a voice that was not as happy as Maggie Rose's. "What do you mean, you're going camping with Dad? Just you?"

Maggie Rose's older brother, Bryan, had come into the room. I ran to sniff Bryan.

"If you're going camping, I want to go, too," Bryan said. "No fair if you get to go and I don't."

"Bryan's right," said another voice. Maggie Rose's oldest brother, Craig, was standing in the doorway, listening to them talk. I went to greet him, and then whipped my head around to stare at my girl.

Something was wrong. Suddenly, just like that, Maggie Rose was not as happy as she'd been a moment ago!

"But Dad said it was just going to be him and me," she said. "You guys are always doing stuff with Dad, and I don't get to go."

"Stuff like what?" Bryan demanded.

I pounced on the old towel and shook it. *This* would make Maggie Rose happy again!

"He goes to your games all the time," she

said, "and takes you to the park to practice soccer and baseball."

"Well, if you did a sport, he'd do that for you, too," Craig pointed out. "You could join the soccer team at school. Or T-ball."

Bryan snorted. "She's too much of a runt to be any good at soccer."

Maggie Rose's back stiffened. I could tell this was some kind of wrestling match going on between her and her brothers. I used to live with my three brothers, before I came to live at Home with my girl, and I remembered wrestling with them.

People sometimes wrestle with words instead of jumping on each other and rolling around in the dirt. I don't really understand how it works, but I can tell when they are wrestling. I can also tell when somebody wins.

Right now, Maggie Rose was wrestling back. But she hadn't won.

"Don't call me a runt," she said. "You're supposed to stop that."

"Yeah, Bryan, knock it off," Craig agreed.

Bryan flopped down on the couch and snorted again.

"And I don't want to play soccer or T-ball. I'm busy most days after school helping Mom at the animal rescue," Maggie Rose went on. "Anyway, I don't see why I should have to play soccer just to spend time with Dad. That's not fair."

"And I don't see why you get some sort of special girl camping trip just for you," Bryan said. "That's not fair, either."

When a dog doesn't understand what people are doing, sometimes the best thing to do is to hunt for treats. I jumped up on the couch to sniff at Bryan's jeans. I could tell that he'd recently had a peanut butter sandwich in one of his pockets.

I pushed my nose as deep into the pocket as

it would go. There was no sandwich in there now, but if I kept sniffing, maybe one would appear.

"Dad!" Bryan called. "Maggie Rose says she's going camping with you."

I pulled my head out of Bryan's pocket to see Dad join us in the living room. I wagged. Mom followed as well, standing just behind Craig in the doorway. She didn't say anything, probably because she was holding a towel. When *I* have a towel, it pretty much takes all my concentration.

"Yes, that's right," Dad agreed.

I could tell that Dad didn't have any peanut butter sandwiches, so I stuck my nose back into Bryan's pocket.

"We want to go, too," Bryan said.

"Yeah, come on, Dad," Craig said. "We haven't been camping since last spring, when it rained the whole time. We should get to go, too. It's not fair if Maggie Rose is the only one."

"But Dad, you said it would just be you and me," Maggie Rose protested.

Her voice sounded so worried that I pulled my head out of Bryan's pocket. I realized I had let her down. To be a good dog, I needed to comfort her, especially since no sandwich had shown up in Bryan's jeans. Something was really bothering her. I jumped to the floor, the peanut butter scent forgotten. Maggie Rose was sitting with her legs crossed. I leaped into her lap and gazed up into her face. What was happening?

"Well," Dad said thoughtfully. "I can see what you boys mean."

"No," my girl moaned. I could see Maggie Rose slump in on herself.

She had lost the wrestling match.

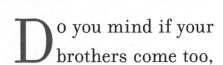

Do you mind if your brothers come too, Maggie Rose?" Dad asked.

"But Dad," Maggie Rose said in a sad, soft voice. "I was hoping it would be a father-daughter camping trip."

Dad frowned. Now something was bothering *him*. "Oh," he said.

Maggie Rose turned her face away. A good dog right there in the room, and everyone was unhappy. No one said anything;

they were probably waiting for me to come up with something cheerful. I should have brought in a stick from the yard!

"I'm sorry, Maggie Rose," Dad said.

My girl sighed. "It's okay," she muttered.

Inspired, I flopped on my back and exposed my tummy. A belly rub makes everyone happy!

Craig stirred. I glanced at him. He was watching Maggie Rose carefully. "You know what?" he said suddenly. "Maybe Maggie Rose is right. She can do a father-daughter trip, and then next time, we can do a father-sons camping trip."

"What?" Bryan demanded.

"Sure. We can go to a movie with Mom or something," Craig continued.

"That could work," Mom agreed. "I have a stray cat coming into the rescue with an eye infection I need to treat, but the rest of my day is free. A movie sounds fun."

Maggie Rose brightened, a small grin on her face. I had done it—I had cheered her up!

"I want to go camping," Bryan insisted stubbornly.

"Come on, Bryan," Craig urged.

"No," Bryan said.

"Let's vote," Maggie Rose suggested.

Dad smiled. "Good idea, Maggie Rose."

I had even made Dad happy!

"Who says this time it's father-daughter?" Craig asked.

Everyone held their hand up in the air, except Bryan. He was the only person I hadn't yet managed to make happy. I went to him and put my nose right in his peanut butter pants.

"And who says it's all of us?" Craig asked.

Bryan lifted his hand in the air, and I gazed up at it curiously. If he thought he was going to throw a ball or something, he was going to be disappointed; his hand was empty.

"All right then, Maggie Rose," Dad said. "Just you and me."

"Yay!" Maggie Rose cheered.

I wagged. What a fun day!

"Let's go do something outside, Bryan," Craig suggested. The two of them left the room. Dad leaned down to pet my head, because I was such a good dog who made everyone happy except Bryan, who maybe just needed a sandwich that I would be willing to help him eat.

"I liked how they handled that them-selves," Mom observed.

"Me, too," Dad replied. Mom turned and went back toward the kitchen, where all the food is, which I thought was a promising de-velopment.

"We have a stop to make along the way," Dad told Maggie Rose. "There's a colony of prairie dogs up near the campground that needs relocating. Someone's putting in a housing development, and the prairie dogs are too close to the new construction. They could get hurt."

My ears perked up and I wagged. There was that word "dogs" again.

"Then we'll head up and pitch a tent, just you and me," Dad concluded.

"And Lily!" Maggie Rose said.

We rolled on the floor and wrestled with the towel some more, and I let her pull it right out of my mouth a few times, so that she'd keep on being that happy.

A few days later, Maggie Rose was very busy putting things into a box made of cloth. She stuffed clothes in there, and her pajamas, and a pair of shoes.

She picked up one of my favorite toys—two old socks that used to belong to Craig before they were mine. They were knotted together to make a long rope.

I lunged. Hooray! We were going to play Pull-on-the-Socks!

I got my teeth into one end of the socks and tugged. Maggie Rose tugged back.

"No, Lily, no!" she kept saying, but she was giggling, so I knew she was as happy to be playing with me as I was to be playing with her. Finally, she whisked the toy out of my mouth.

"No, Lily—I'm trying to pack it in the suit-case, so we'll have something for you to play with!" she told me, and she stuffed the socks into the cloth box along with all the other things.

I sat and stared in confusion. How could we tug on a sock if she was going to put it in that box?

But I soon forgot about it, because Maggie Rose called me out for a car ride in the truck. Rides with my girl are one of my favorite things. Dad sat in the front of the truck. In the back, Maggie Rose rolled the window down a little, so that I could put my nose to the crack and sniff and sniff and sniff.

At first I smelled the city—cars and trucks, with their sour odors of smoke and metal and hot oil; pavement; and all sorts of people living close together, lots with food smells on them. There were dogs, too, and many other animals. The city packed all of these scents into one thick, dense smell.

We drove for a while, and the houses started to be spaced farther and

farther apart. There were more trees and wider stretches of grass. There were more animals out here, too, not just dogs. Sometimes we passed horses or cows in fields, who just stared in jealousy that there was a dog in a car staring back; and sometimes there were other animals that I could not see but only smell, faint on the air.

"I can't wait to see the prairie dogs. They're so cute!" Maggie Rose said eagerly.

Dad nodded. "I think so, too. But they can be a problem."

"What kind of problem?" Maggie Rose asked. "They're so little. It's not like they can hurt somebody."

"Actually, they can," Dad said. "They carry fleas, and fleas can carry diseases. So you and Lily should both stay in the truck."

I put my head in Maggie Rose's lap with a long sigh of contentment.

I love my girl.

"Prairie dogs live in family groups—coteries—so there can be a lot of them. And they're rodents.

They eat seeds and grasses, mostly. They dig tunnels underground. Most people don't want a prairie dog tunnel under their lawn. Or under a field. Sometimes a horse will slip into a prairie dog hole and break a leg."

"Well, maybe people shouldn't build houses where prairie dogs live, then!" Maggie Rose declared, a little fiercely.

Dad shook his head. "Well, people want houses, Maggie. We live in a house, don't we? And horses and cows need fields. What we've got to do—what it's my job to do—is balance out the needs. Try and find a safe place for animals, where they're not going to create a problem for people."

"So we're going to catch them and set them free somewhere else?" Maggie Rose asked.

Dad nodded. "That's the idea. The problem, though, is that prairie dogs are really hard to round up. Today we're going to try something new. If it works, we'll have a safe way to catch them."

"What if it doesn't work?" Maggie Rose asked anxiously. I wagged, thinking that if she was worried about something, we should get Craig's socks out of the cloth box.

Dad didn't answer right away. Then he gave Maggie Rose a serious look. "If this doesn't work, I am not sure we can save the prairie dogs."

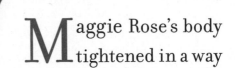

Maggie Rose's body tightened in a way I knew was a mixture of angry and afraid. I nosed her hand. Dad glanced at her again. "Oh, sorry, honey. I didn't mean to upset you. I think we're going to be fine. Basically, we're going to catch the prairie dogs by vacuum suction."

"What?" Maggie Rose spluttered. She sounded so surprised that I cocked my head at her, staring into her face. "You're going to vacuum up the prairie dogs?" she asked. "Like with a vacuum cleaner?"

I could tell from Dad's voice that he was amused. "Sort of. It's a new technology. It used to be there was no safe way to get rid of a prairie dog coterie. People would have to shoot them or poison them—"

"No!" Maggie Rose cried out.

"Right. No good," Dad agreed. "So someone came up with this idea. It really is a lot like a giant vacuum cleaner. There's a hose that goes into the tunnel and just sucks the prairie dogs right out and into a padded cage."

"Doesn't it hurt them?" Maggie Rose asked. She sounded a little anxious, and I licked her hands to reassure her. "I wouldn't like it if someone pulled the roof off my house and sucked me up!"

"Well, I'm sure it's scary for them," Dad said. "That's partly why I'm going, to make sure no animals get hurt. If it seems too rough, I'll put a stop to it. But if it works, it's really the best thing. Getting the prairie dogs away from humans means everybody can live in peace. So let's cross our fingers."

Maggie Rose still seemed worried. I could not understand it at all. Both of them kept saying "dog," so we must have been going somewhere fun. Probably a dog park! What was there to be worried about in a dog park?

But when the truck came to a stop and Dad climbed out, Maggie Rose and I stayed in the back seat. So clearly, we were not at a dog park at all. I never have to stay in the car at a dog park.

At least Maggie Rose opened the windows so I could see and smell. She clicked my leash on my collar, though, and held it so that I could not jump out.

There were several people walking around outside, and I wanted to sniff them all and make new friends. Also, there was a fascinating smell drifting toward me on the breeze. Somewhere close by was a completely new animal I had never met before.

I wanted to meet that animal very much. I am very good at meeting animals! I have met a crow named Casey and two pigs and a squirrel, plus so many dogs and cats I have lost count. And a ferret named Freddie, of course. They are all my friends.

When was I going to get a chance to make friends with this new animal?

The people gathered together in groups and talked, and then they walked around and talked some more. I looked up at Maggie Rose and whined so that she'd know to let me out.

Maggie Rose stroked my back. "No, Lily," she said. "We have to stay here."

I do not like that word, "no."

I perked up; the field was littered with mounds of dirt with holes in them, and for just a moment a small head poked up and then vanished back down. *This* was the new animal I could smell so strongly!

Two of the men outside stuck a long hose into a hole in the ground. The other end of the hose went into a truck that was parked right next to ours. The back of the truck had a big window set into one side so that I could see right into it. I yawned, not understanding anything.

"Ready!" someone shouted. Then there was a very loud, rumbling *whoosh*. I jumped, startled, and tried to shake the sound out of my ears. I wished it would stop, but it just went on and on!

Dad turned and looked back at

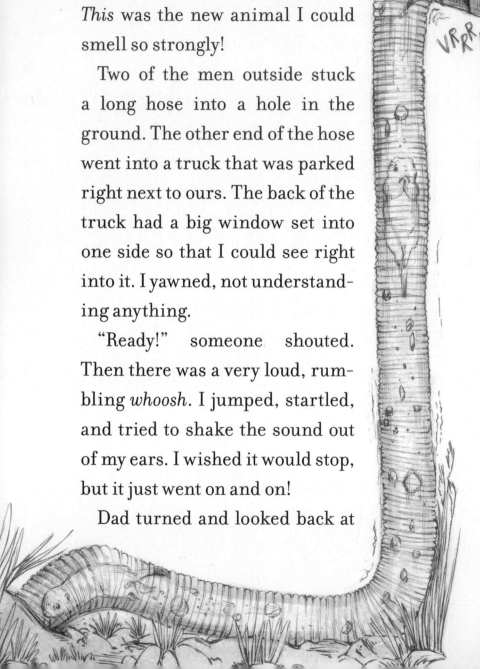

VRRRR

VRRRR

us, probably wondering why we didn't jump
out and run around. He shook his head and
raised his hands.

"Oh no—he says it isn't working, Lily!"
Maggie Rose moaned.

I looked at my girl. Whatever we were doing was not making her happy. I tried to
think of what I could do, but all I could think
of was chicken treats.

"Got one!" shouted a voice. "There it goes!"

Maggie Rose squirmed nearer to the window. "Lily, look!"

I had no idea what she was talking about, though I wagged a little to hear my name. Suddenly, to my surprise, I caught a glimpse of something moving inside the truck near ours. Through the big window, I could see a small furry body drop through the air and plop onto the floor. It immediately jumped up and glanced around. It looked like a big squirrel! As far as I could tell without smelling it, it seemed very surprised.

"They vacuumed one up!" Maggie Rose told me excitedly.

4

The squirrel in the back of the truck was sniffing at the floor, maybe looking for peanuts. This was a new type of squirrel to me, and I wagged, thinking how much fun we were going to have when Maggie Rose let me join it in the big truck with the window! A moment later it was joined by another, and then another. They all touched noses, like dogs in a dog park, but they did not sniff each other's butts.

"It's like a bounce house!" Maggie Rose told me. She clapped her hands together. She was grinning. "A prairie dog bounce house. Do you think they like bounce houses as much as I do, Lily?"

Yes, I thought to myself. If we weren't going to have chicken treats, I was ready to play with the new squirrels.

Pretty soon, the loud noise stopped. I was relieved. Dad returned to the truck, smiling.

"Got them all, I think," he told Maggie Rose. "No injuries. Looks like this is really going to work!"

Now everyone was happy! This is one of the main jobs of being a dog, and I was glad I had managed to cheer everyone up. I thought it would be an excellent time to break out Craig's socks. A man and a woman, both wearing thick gloves, climbed into the truck where the small plump squirrels had landed. I wished I could go in there, too. I would love to play Chase-Me in a truck full of squirrels!

But it seemed that no one was thinking about how much a good dog would like to play Chase-Me, because in a little while our truck was moving again, and so was the truck with the big windows. They were taking the new squirrels for a car ride!

I squirmed around in Maggie Rose's arms to watch out the back window. She unsnapped my leash so I could move more easily.

I was not sure what we were doing. If these squirrels were going for a car ride, why couldn't they be here in the back seat with my girl and me? We could all sniff out the windows.

"Next stop: a new home for prairie dogs!" Dad said to Maggie Rose.

I wagged. Dad sounded so happy that a dog park seemed like a real possibility!

Finally, the truck came to a stop. We were in

a grassy field. A couple of other cars bumped down the road after us and stopped nearby.

I looked eagerly at Maggie Rose, wagging as hard as I could. We were going to get out now, right? And run with the squirrels?

"Is this where the prairie dogs are going to live, Dad?" Maggie Rose asked.

Dad nodded. "I came out here with some other wardens a couple of days ago, and we dug a new burrow for them," he said. "They need someplace to hide, or hawks or ferrets could get them."

"Ferrets like Freddie? At the shelter?" Maggie Rose asked. "I've never seen Freddie try to hunt any of the other animals. He's friends with Lily!"

Dad put his hand on my head, smoothing my fur, and I wagged. "Sure, but a tame ferret in a cage isn't the same as a wild one, honey," Dad said. "Freddie gets fed every day, so he doesn't have to hunt. There are wild ones out here, though, and prairie dog is on their menu. But with a tunnel to dive into, these little guys should be safe. Let's see how they like their new home!"

Then Dad climbed out, but to my surprise, Maggie Rose didn't. She didn't let me out, either. I barked at the windows to remind her that I had been a good dog in the car for a very long time, and I needed to run around. Peeing would be nice, too. But she didn't open the door. She did, however, lower my window all the way, so I could drink in all the wonderful odors.

Dad walked around to the back of the squirrel truck. He and a woman held sticks with big nets on the end. When he opened the back of the truck, the new squirrels scampered and squeaked inside their room. They seemed unhappy.

Clearly, they needed a good dog to cheer them up. I looked impatiently at Maggie Rose.

When was she going to let me out of the car?

I didn't understand what was going on! Dad and the woman began gently thrusting their sticks into the back of the truck, pulling out netfuls of squirrels. The two humans set all the squirrels on the ground and the little creatures immediately took off running, as if playing Chase-Me. They ran a very short distance to some mounds of dirt. They sniffed the dirt, but mostly they sniffed each other. They seemed confused, which I understood—how do you play Chase-Me without a dog?

Dad came back to us. "They've found the prairie dog town, but they don't want to go in the tunnels for some reason. We're going to have to chase them into the holes, get them used to the idea!"

I wagged.

Dad stood and watched as the rest of the people moved slowly, walking around the confused pack of new squirrels. He groaned when a good number of the little animals started doing the game correctly, dashing a short distance out into the open fields. "Stop!" he called. "This is just making this worse!"

I simply couldn't understand it. The squirrels had bunched up, sniffing each other, trying to figure out when I would come out and play. The people had stopped moving and were standing around with their hands on their hips.

"Laurie," Dad called, "go way around, out

into the field, cut off their escape that way. This is a disaster—we need to get them into the holes! But they have never seen people, and don't understand what we are."

I saw a woman run away and then, after a few moments, curve around until she wound up standing far out in the grass, between us and the squirrels. They saw her, too: they stood up on their rear legs, trying to see what she was up to.

I couldn't wait any longer. I squirmed and twisted and slipped out of Maggie Rose's hands. Then I leaped for the open window.

Time to play!

"Lily, come back!" Maggie Rose shrieked.

5

As soon as I hit the ground, I started running straight toward the cluster of squirrels, so happy to finally be playing! They reacted by milling around for a moment and then dashing in all directions.

"No, Lily!" Maggie Rose wailed.

I was almost on top of a squirrel, and then it vanished! It had darted down into a hole. I turned to pursue another, and it dove into the ground as well. What? These squirrels

weren't climbing trees, but they were playing unfairly anyway. Within moments, they
were all gone!

I always think squirrels are going to do
Chase-Me correctly, but I get fooled every
time.

Dad came over and reached down and I
wagged. He picked me up in his big, thick
gloves and carried me over to the truck.
"Well, I should be angry with you that you

lct Lily escape," he told Maggie Rose as she opened the door, "but it turns out she was just what we needed. The prairie dogs didn't understand when they saw people coming to try to herd them, but they recognized a predator when they saw one, and followed their instincts right into their new homes!"

"Oh, Lily would never hurt any of them."

"Right," Dad agreed. "But they don't know that."

Dad took me to the back of the truck, raised the door, and pulled out a hose.

"What are you doing?" my girl asked him.

"I don't think Lily has any fleas on her, but we can't take that chance. I have flea shampoo, and I am going to bathe her right now with this water tank I always carry."

I was wagging until Dad started giving me a bath, and then I was not wagging. A bath? After I had been such a good dog?

Sometimes I just do not understand people.

Dad used miserably stinky liquid on me, and I sneezed, and then he poured water on me and toweled me down. I liked the towel but nothing else. Finally, he took me to Maggie Rose and laid me in her lap.

"I'm watching the prairie dogs, Dad! They keep coming up to look around, and a couple are digging in the grass," Maggie Rose said as Dad started the truck.

"It worked like a charm. Great to have a new way of moving those little guys without hurting them!" Dad said happily.

I settled onto Maggie Rose's lap for a nap, but I woke up when the truck stopped. I figured we were Home again, or maybe at Work, where I have so many friends—Brewster the dog, Freddie the ferret, and all the other cats and dogs who visit for a while and then leave with their new people.

But where we were—it did not smell like Home or Work. The scent of this place wafted in through the open windows, and it smelled full of plants and living things. It smelled *wild*.

"Come and see the campsite, Lily!" Maggie Rose said, and she held the door open for me.

We were on a small, flat patch of ground surrounded by trees—towering trees, more and bigger than I had ever seen in one place before. Through a couple of the trees I could see and smell a big patch of water. Next to us was the truck, and a sooty circle surrounded by rocks, and a flat table with benches alongside it, and a strange sort of house made of cloth that Dad was tugging on.

What *was* this place?

Nose to the dirt, I dashed around eagerly, pulling Maggie Rose behind me on my leash. Other people had walked over this area, but not very many. More animals than people had been here. Some of the scents I recognized, like squirrels (tree squirrels, not hole-in-the-ground squirrels) and deer.

Were we going to stay here? Was this our new Home? What about Mom and Bryan and Craig? What about Work, with all my animal friends? Wouldn't they miss me? I would certainly miss them!

"Oh, Lily, you look worried," Maggie Rose said. She got down on her knees to scratch my back and rub my ears. "Don't worry, you'll like camping. It's going to be fun. Fun, Lily!"

So then I knew that, whatever was happening, it was going to be good. Maggie Rose was happy. That proved it.

"I feel kind of bad that the boys don't get to see this," Maggie Rose said, looking up at Dad. "They would really love this place."

Dad had some big pieces of wood in his arms. He dropped them next to the sooty circle on the ground.

"You've got a big heart, Maggie Rose," he said. "And we'll come back with the boys another day. But this time is for you and me."

I gnawed on a stick while Maggie Rose and Dad pulled things from the car and put them inside the cloth house. Then Dad played with his wood that he had put in the sooty circle on the ground. Before too long, the sharp smell of smoke pushed up into the air, with bright flames licking out from the sticks.

Sometimes at Home I had seen a fire in the fireplace, but this was new! It seemed more exciting to have a fire out in the open, not stuck behind a screen in the wall. We were having a wonderful time, even if I wasn't sure what we were doing. I sat and scratched behind my ear with a rear paw.

I *really* liked the open fire when Maggie Rose and Dad put hot dogs on sticks and stuck them into the flames. That smelled so marvelous that I drooled in the dirt! I sat

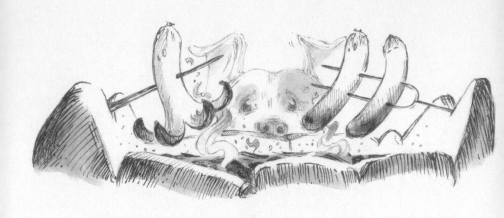

and watched intently as Maggie Rose put her hot dog in bread, sprayed it with something that had a sweet odor, and began eating.

I concentrated on staring at Maggie Rose, letting her know with my gaze that I would very much appreciate a piece of hot dog. I was being a good dog. Would she give me one?

6

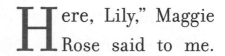

"Here, Lily," Maggie Rose said to me. She extended a big chunk of hot dog toward me, and I delicately lifted it from her fingers. This was how I knew my girl loved me, and that I was indeed a good dog who deserved a piece of hot dog, and hopefully another one.

After the sky turned dark, Dad and Maggie Rose and I climbed inside the cloth house.

It was a strange place! There were no beds. Maggie Rose lay down on the floor and snuggled into a silky kind of blanket that was a little like the bags Mom and Dad carried food in. Dad lay down beside her in his own bag. There was no bag for a dog.

I was so puzzled I flung myself on my girl, panting into her face.

"Ugh, Lily, calm down!" Maggie Rose said. She put an arm around me and tugged me down between her and Dad. "You sleep here, okay, Lily? Sleep right here."

Maggie Rose lay still, and after a while I could tell from her breathing that she was sleeping. Dad, too.

But I was wide awake. All the smells of the outdoors came drifting into the cloth house, and I could hear birds calling, small animals scurrying, and something bigger clomping through the bushes.

I squirmed up to lick Maggie Rose's face, wanting her awake so that she could experience all this with me.

"Mmmmmph. Lily. No," Maggie Rose said sleepily.

That word again. "No." I licked Maggie Rose's ear. Why wouldn't she wake up? Surely we weren't going to just lie here, with all the animal scents and sounds on the other side of the cloth walls.

"Lily. Sleep. Now," Maggie Rose mumbled.

So I had to lie there, the only one awake.

What was going on?

In the morning I decided my confusion didn't matter, because everything was so much fun!

First, Dad cooked breakfast over the fire. Maggie Rose put my regular food in my bowl for me, but she also let me have some of her scrambled eggs with bacon. The bacon was a little burned, but I did not care at all. I will eat bacon under all circumstances.

Then she took me for a walk in the woods,

but she did not put on my leash. And I had never smelled so many interesting smells in one place. Rocks! Moss! Leaves! Sticks! Animal poop!

And even more exciting were the animals who had left the poop. Animal scents were everywhere! They had walked over the ground, and they had left scratches in the dirt and pee under the bushes.

I could hardly believe how marvelous it was! Yes, I missed Mom and Casey and Brewster and Craig and Bryan with his peanut butter pockets, but this place was the best, and as far as I was concerned they should all come to live with us here and sleep in the cloth room.

The only thing that could have made it better was if some of these animals had come out to play. But they seemed to be shy. Some animals are shy at first, but I've made friends with nearly all of them in the end. If

they became really good friends, I thought,
they could sleep in the cloth room with the
rest of us.

Maggie Rose led me down a path toward the
glimmering water I had glimpsed yesterday.

I was surprised when we arrived there. I was used to seeing the water in my bowl, and I'd watched Maggie Rose fill up the tub at Home with water and get in it. That was called a "bath," and I usually left the room as soon as I heard the word, because I did not want to get involved in such matters. My girl's bathwater had bubbles in it that smelled strange and tasted worse. My baths, like the one I'd just had, had fewer bubbles and smelled absolutely awful.

There is no reason for anyone to ever take a bath that a dog can understand.

This water, though, was different. For one thing, it was huge! There was much more water than would ever fit into my bowl, or even into Maggie Rose's tub.

It did not have bubbles in it, either. Instead, there were plants growing in it. I took a tentative drink, then returned to my girl's side. Then, in the bushes behind her,

I caught a new scent. I stopped and sniffed hard.

An animal! A new friend! I could hear it now. It made a rustling sound. It was coming closer! It had stopped being shy and was ready to play!

A slender, dark head with two glistening eyes poked out of the bush behind Maggie Rose. My new friend was small, about the same size as Freddie, my friend the ferret, and I could smell that she was female. I could also smell that she was not a dog. As she emerged from the shrubs, I saw that she was all black, except for two long white stripes down her back.

Another new type of squirrel? I already knew that dogs came in all sizes and shapes, but I'd never before considered that squirrels might try to be like dogs, and be different from each other as well.

A striped squirrel! How exciting! Maybe

this one would play Chase-Me fairly. I bowed down with my front legs low, my rump high, and my tail waving, to let my new squirrel friend know I was ready.

The squirrel made a funny kind of grunting sound, turned, and waddled back into the bush.

Time to chase!

"Lily! Where are you going?" Maggie Rose shouted as I plowed through the bush. "Come back! That's a skunk!"

7

Twigs and leaves slapped me, but I struggled through. On the other side, right by a mossy log, was my new friend. She peered at me and then turned so her butt was facing me.

Obviously, this was a squirrel who understood the polite way to introduce herself to a dog. I wanted to be polite as well, so I trotted up to give her butt a good sniff. My new friend lifted up her tail so I could smell better. This

was also new information, that some squir
rels wanted so much to be like dogs that they
had learned how to act like us.

I could hear Maggie Rose trying to come
through the bush after us. "Dad! Lily ran
after a skunk!" she called.

"No, Lily!" Dad shouted.

Why would anyone say "No!" about meeting a new friend? People should really think

harder about how they use that word. Other than "bath," it was the worst thing humans could ever say. I sniffed my new friend's butt more deeply.

"Call her! We can't let her get sprayed by that skunk, Maggie Rose!" Dad yelled.

"Lily, come here! Get away from the skunk!" my girl called out.

There were two words in that sentence that I knew—"Lily" and "come." And Maggie Rose was saying a new word I had never heard before. Dad had said that word, too.

"Skunk." They were saying "skunk."

Perhaps they meant that my new friend was called skunk, not squirrel. Maybe that's why it didn't run up a tree or down a hole or into a giant hose.

I left the skunk and ran toward my girl, because she'd said "come." I always go to her when she says that.

Well, most of the time.

Some of the time, anyway.

Oddly, as I approached, wagging happily, Maggie Rose did not seem glad to see me. She backed away as I came closer. What was wrong?

"Great," Dad groaned. "Lily got sprayed by that skunk. Take her down to the pond, Maggie Rose. I've still got some shampoo in the truck. I'll go fetch it. You get her fur wet. But try not to let her rub against you, or we'll have to clean you, too."

"Come on, Lily," Maggie Rose urged, moving backward toward the big water. "Lily, follow me—no, don't touch me!" She skipped out of my way. "Come, Lily!"

This was an extremely confusing game. She was calling me, but then when I obeyed, she said "no." Did she want me close to her or not? But I followed her, because she's my girl.

Maggie Rose kicked off her shoes and

waded right into the water. I sat on the shore and watched curiously. She waded up to her knees and then called to me. "Lily, come!"

So now she wanted me near her again. I splashed happily into the water.

Maggie Rose backed away from me. "It's so cold!" she exclaimed. She scooped up a handful of water and tossed it at me. "Better get you wet. Here, Lily! We need to give you a bath!"

I froze. A bath? Another *bath*? Was that why we were here? That couldn't be true, could it?

I shook my head to get rid of the water and spotted something floating right behind my girl. A stick! A stick would take her mind off the whole bath subject. I lunged at it. It felt funny, trying to run in the heavy water. I pushed through it and heaved myself forward.

Suddenly there was no more sand under

my paws. It had dropped away, and all I could touch was water. It was like jumping into one of the holes Craig and Bryan sometimes dug in the field.

I was sinking.

This was very interesting. I had never been underneath water before. I kept trying to run, but my running was not taking me anywhere. My paws brushed pebbles and then I was standing, looking up, where the sun was acting very crazy, dancing and bobbing at the surface of the water.

I could faintly hear Maggie Rose calling, "Lily! Lily!" I hoped she would soon realize that I couldn't run to her. I was a good dog who always came when I was called, but not now!

I couldn't even really see my girl.

I couldn't smell her.

I could hardly hear her.

I saw her wobble and jump as she waded toward me. My girl's hands plunged through the clear water to grab me and pull me up to the surface. "Lily! I've got you!" she gasped.

She held me tight to her chest. She was struggling, as if she were trying to run just as I had been. But she wasn't getting anywhere.

The water was nearly over my head. Only my nose and eyes were out. I was glad about my nose, because I realized now that I had not been able to breathe during that underwater time.

Maggie Rose was up to her neck, too. Her head was tipped back in the water so that just her face was out. "Dad!" she shouted.

Dad came running down the path and leaped into the water with us. Now we were all playing this strange water game.

People usually decide what dogs are going to do, but in my opinion, there are other games that are more fun. Like Chase-Me. Or Pull-on-Craig's-Socks.

Dad grabbed Maggie Rose and me together. "I've got you both." He picked us up and carried us to the shore. Then he sat down on a big log with my girl on his lap, hugging her.

I squirmed away and ran in a few circles and tried to shake the water out of my fur. What were we going to do next? Maybe it would involve bacon.

My girl was shivering. "You're okay. You're okay," Dad told her. "Lily's okay, too."

"I was scared," Maggie Rose replied weakly. "Lily just sank. I thought she'd dog paddle."

"Not all dogs can swim," Dad told her. "Lily's a pit bull mix, and pits are pretty heavy. All that muscle. They can't float, so some of them can't doggy paddle. Don't go in after her again, Maggie Rose, hear me? Call for me. Got it?"

Maggie Rose nodded.

Dad hugged her tightly. Then he laughed just a little bit. "Great. We're all going to smell like skunk now."

Maggie Rose laughed a little, too.

I wagged.

Dad lifted his hands to his face and smelled them.

He frowned.

Dad put his face in Maggie Rose's hair and inhaled deeply through his nose.

This was interesting! I watched closely. I have never understood why people do not sniff things more. They miss so many wonderful scents.

"You don't smell like skunk, either," he said. "Lily! Lily, come!"

Maggie Rose wiggled off of Dad's lap, and

I trotted over to him. Maybe it would be my turn on Dad's lap now.

But Dad put out a hand to stop me before I could snuggle. He put his nose in my fur. He sniffed. I wagged and sniffed him back. I wondered if I should turn around so he could sniff under my tail.

"No skunk smell at all!" Dad declared.

"Maybe the skunk missed Lily?" Maggie Rose suggested.

"Couldn't have. She had her nose right in the skunk's butt, and I saw it lift up its tail and aim right at her. Your dog should have gotten a full blast of skunk right in her face. A skunk's spray is the only way it can protect itself. They're not fast, they don't have big teeth, and they can't climb trees. All they can do is squirt that awful smell. And it works! Even bigger animals will back right off if a skunk lifts up its tail. So how come Lily doesn't stink?"

My girl was shivering. "I don't know."

"You're both way too cold to sit around talking about skunks!" Dad decided. "Come on. We've got to get you dry."

We went back to the place where we'd spent the night, and Dad put more wood on the fire. I wagged, remembering the bacon from breakfast. Maggie Rose crawled into the cloth house and came out again with dry clothes on. She carried a towel that she used to rub me all over.

It felt good! I wiggled and jumped. But I was still trembling, and Maggie Rose was, too.

"Sit right by the fire," Dad said. "Here." He went into the cloth house, too, and came out with a blanket that he wrapped around my girl.

"But what about Lily?" Maggie Rose asked. "She's cold, too."

"She's got fur. She'll be okay."

Maggie Rose thought for a moment. "I know!" She shook off the blanket and climbed into the cloth house. Was this a new people game, crawling in and out of the cloth house? She came back out with a puffy coat in her hand. She draped the coat over my back. Then she picked up my front legs, one at a time, and stuffed them into the arms of the coat.

I let her do this, because I love her. Then I stood up and shook as hard as I could.

The coat did not fall off. But the hood flopped forward over my eyes. I shook my head hard to make it go away. It only flopped down farther until it hung over my nose.

My girl was giggling. Dad was laughing, too.

None of this could possibly make sense to a dog.

Dad said, "Once you two are all warmed up, there's something we've got to do."

"What, Dad?" Maggie Rose asked.

"Find that skunk."

In a little while, Maggie Rose figured out that I did not want to be in her coat and took it off me. She rubbed her hair hard with the towel and hung it up on a rope stretched between two trees. "Ready!" she told Dad.

"Great," Dad said. "If that skunk actually

can't spray, it can't defend itself. And we can't leave it out here like that. So let's see if Lily can track it down."

"Find the skunk, Lily!" Maggie Rose said to me.

I sat down on the ground and looked up at her. What game were we playing now?

Maggie Rose hurried off down the path toward the water. I followed, of course. When she reached the bush where I had met my black-and-white friend, she stopped. She pointed at the thick shrubs.

"Skunk, Lily!" she said. "Find the skunk!"

Clearly, Maggie Rose wanted me to do something. I tried to think what that might be. Some sort of treat would probably help me figure it out. That bacon would be best.

"Find the skunk!"

Skunk. She and Dad had said that word earlier, before Maggie Rose and I had played the strange game in the water. Were we play-ing another game now?

The way Maggie Rose was saying "find the skunk!" reminded me of being in the back-yard, when she would say, "find the ball!" When she said that, I would run around un-til I found a ball and bring it to her.

Maybe I was supposed to find the skunk!

No, that didn't seem right. I gazed at my girl's face.

"Find the skunk! The skunk!" she urged.

I'd never heard "skunk" before, and now it seemed like all anyone wanted to say. I looked around. No skunk. I poked my head into the bush. I couldn't see any skunk there, either.

But I could smell it. I put my nose down to the ground and sniffed. I pushed through the shrubs and followed the skunk's trail, right to the mossy log where I had been treated to a good sniff of her butt. When I had left to play in the water with Maggie Rose, the skunk had climbed over the log and wandered off among the trees.

I clambered right over the log and followed her scent trail.

9

Maggie Rose and Dad followed me as I tracked that skunk across the dirt, around trees, and through patches of dry grass. We were all playing Chase-the-Skunk!

I hoped skunks understood Chase-Me better than squirrels did, and that the skunk would not ruin the game by running up a tree or down a hole or into a loud hose.

There were many interesting animal scents distracting me from that skunk, now that I had my nose to the ground. My girl and Dad were having trouble keeping up, so I felt free to check some of them out. Wait, what was this? A male dog had been here recently. I sniffed carefully.

"Lily! Find the skunk!" Maggie Rose said urgently as she came up behind me.

"Did you lose the trail, Lily?" Dad asked.

I heard my name, and I heard "skunk," which reminded me what we were doing. I plunged off again. I felt a bit like a bad dog for having stopped to sniff the male dog scent, but it was actually his fault, not mine. Male dogs just don't always understand what is important.

I was getting closer, I could tell—the skunk smell was so strong now that I knew Maggie Rose and Dad could probably smell her as well. Should I wait and let them find the skunk, instead?

I was going to do just that when I scrambled over a thick root and plopped down on the other side. There she was! The skunk!

She was clawing at a rotten log on the ground. She stuck her face into the crumbled bit of wood and snapped up something wiggly between her teeth.

Then she saw me. She lifted her tail high, lowered her head, and shifted her weight from foot to foot. She wanted to play! I should have brought Craig's socks.

The skunk backed up and spun around to show me her butt. I'd already sniffed it once, but I didn't want to be rude, so I did it again.

Dad and Maggie Rose were right behind me. I glanced over and saw Dad take something out of Maggie Rose's backpack—a sort of thin cloth net. He threw it forward. It had a weight at each corner, so it flattened out as it sailed through the air.

The net flopped to the ground over the skunk and me, covering us both.

Today I'd had a coat on me, and now I was wearing a net. This was very strange, and not how I usually played.

Enough light was coming through the thin cloth that I could still see the skunk. She did not seem happy. I could tell that she was startled and afraid and she wanted to run, but the net was trapping us both.

I wagged at the skunk, so she'd know we were friends. She backed away from me a little, but she didn't have much space to move.

"Stay there," I heard Dad tell Maggie Rose. Then he came closer. In a moment his big hands pushed through the cloth and scooped that skunk right up—still wrapped tight in the thin net.

I was concerned for my new friend. I wished I knew a way to tell her that, with Dad holding her, she was safe.

The skunk wriggled and bit at the net as Dad carried her to the back of the truck.

I followed, my nose up to smell my new
friend. Dad lifted the back of the truck and
opened the dog crate there. He plopped the
skunk inside, pulled away the thin netting,
and shut the door.

"Phew!" Dad said. "That went easier than
I expected."

"Can we put Lily in the back, too? She always helps with scared animals," my girl
asked. I wagged at my name.

"Well, sure—we can try it, but if it makes

the situation worse, we'll need to pull your dog right back out."

Dad lifted me up and set me next to the dog crate. I peered in through the wire mesh door. The skunk was huddled in a corner. I could tell she was in no mood to play. Sometimes it's like that when I meet new friends.

I flopped down near the crate so that the skunk would see I was no threat. I watched her carefully to see if she understood.

"Look how calm Lily is," Dad said. He sounded a little surprised. "I think she's actually helping the skunk stay calm, too."

"Of course Lily's helping," said Maggie Rose. "She's a rescue dog. It's what she does."

"She's amazing," Dad said. "Maggie Rose, I'm afraid we have to cut our camping trip short. We've got to get this skunk down to your mother. She can tell if the skunk really can't spray scent. If she can't, maybe there's something your mom can do."

"What if Mom can't fix it?" my girl wondered.

Dad was silent for a moment. "Then I don't know if there's anything to help the skunk, honey."

"Mom will fix it," my girl said urgently. "She *has* to!"

Maggie Rose and Dad became very busy, packing things and moving them and putting them in the back of the truck. Dad picked up the box with the bacon in it, and even though we could all smell it in there, he didn't offer me any, which I found baffling.

After it was all over, Maggie Rose reached over and lifted me away from the skunk.

I whined a little. I could tell the skunk was still afraid, and I did not like to leave a new friend who was frightened and alone.

Maggie Rose carried me around to the back seat of the truck and climbed in with me. Another car ride!

I hoped that my new skunk friend liked car rides as much as I did.

10

The skunk did not like the car ride. I could smell her back there in the crate, and she smelled like fear.

We drove all the way to Work. I love Work! On most of the days when Maggie Rose says, "I have to go to school now. Bye, Lily!" I go to Work with Mom.

At Work there are lots of other animals—dogs and cats and kittens and puppies. Once a crow came to stay with us. His name is Casey, and he became one of my best friends.

Another friend is an old dog named Brewster, who is probably the best nap-taker I have ever met.

I wondered what games I would play with my new friend the skunk. So far she had only seemed interested in Sniff-My-Butt.

Dad carried the skunk into Work and put the crate down on the floor. Then he and Mom talked while Maggie Rose and I listened carefully to see if any treats were mentioned. Mom put on a pair of heavy gloves and knelt down to open up the skunk's crate. She reached in and wrapped up the skunk in a piece of thick, tough cloth.

I wondered why both Mom and Dad seemed to think it was a good idea to play a game called Wrap-the-Skunk.

The skunk squirmed and tried to bite. I could smell that she was very frightened. "She's a young one," Mom remarked. Maggie Rose and I waited while Mom looked at the skunk very carefully.

"I think you are exactly right," Mom said to Dad with a sigh. Very gently, she put the skunk back into her crate and pulled away the sheet. "She has no scent glands. As far as I can tell, she was born that way."

"She can't spray?" Dad asked.

Mom shook her head. "She's a stinkless skunk."

Dad's shoulders slumped. "That means she has no defenses at all. There's no way she can survive in the wild."

Maggie Rose took me near the skunk's crate. She set me down. "Go on, Lily," she whispered to me. "Do your job. Make her feel better."

I put my nose to the crate door. I sniffed. The skunk stayed far back in a corner and did not come to touch noses with me.

This was bad. This skunk was very afraid.

Dad started talking to his phone, and Mom went to a desk to look at some papers. Humans like looking at papers. I do not know why. They don't smell or taste interesting at all. Maggie Rose went to the back door and opened it, and wonderful scents drifted in on the warm air. My girl raised her face to the sun and closed her eyes and smiled.

There was a rustle of wings in the air, and something flew in through the open door and landed on top of my head. I felt claws pricking through my fur.

"Ree-ree," a voice croaked. "Ree-ree."

It was my friend Casey! Crows can talk better than dogs, but not as well as people. "Ree-ree" was his way of saying "Lily." Or maybe it was his way of saying "Hello." Or "We should have chicken treats." I am a dog and have too many things going on to try to learn how to understand bird. But I was very happy, and I wagged.

Casey sometimes likes to take rides on my head, so I circled the skunk's crate. Then I went back to the crate door.

The skunk had stirred from her corner. She had come over to the door, and was crouching down low to see what was happening.

Probably she had never seen a crow ride on a dog's head before. A lot of people—and animals, too—are interested when Casey and I do this.

I sat down. Casey stayed on my head. He leaned forward a bit to peer at the skunk. The skunk peered back.

I hoped the skunk was starting to understand that living at Work would be fun. She would get to play with Casey. She would get to play with me. She could nap with Brewster.

"Look, Mom," Maggie Rose said softly. "Lily's doing her job, and Casey's helping!"

"You're right," Mom said, just as softly.

"I've never seen a wild animal calm down so quickly. Sometimes when animals are frightened, seeing something completely unexpected takes their mind off what's scaring them. Like a bird on a dog's head!"

Mom picked up the skunk, and I followed her as she took the little crate inside a kennel. Kennels have a cement floor, a bed to lie on, and dishes full of food.

Mom left me with the skunk crate in the kennel, shutting the gate behind her. What were we doing now?

Casey had flown off my head by then, but he flapped over to the kennel and gripped the wires with both feet so he could gaze down at the skunk. He was as interested as I was.

"Keep an eye on them, Maggie Rose," Mom said. "Don't open the crate, though. Just because that skunk can't spray you doesn't mean she can't bite you."

I sat down beside the crate. Being inside the kennel made me remember my early days, when I had lived in a kennel like this with my mother and my three brothers. That was before I went Home to live with Maggie Rose.

I guessed that the skunk would do the same thing. She would live here in the kennel for a while, and then she'd go Home with us. We'd both eat out of our bowls in the kitchen, and sleep pressed against Maggie Rose's legs in her bed.

"Stinkerbelle," Maggie Rose said to Dad later. "I'm going to name the skunk Stinkerbelle."

"That's a good name," Dad said with a smile.

"If Stinkerbelle can't live in the wild, what are we going to do with her?"

"I don't know, Maggie Rose. I just don't know."

11

Every day at Work, Maggie Rose would let me into the skunk's kennel. My girl called the skunk Stinkerbelle, so I knew that was the skunk's name. People always know names, even before the animals themselves do. I didn't know I was Lily until Maggie Rose told me.

Inside the kennel was the skunk's crate. The door was open. Stinkerbelle seemed curious about me, but not enough to come out right away. Sometimes she sniffed out the open door, watching me. Casey was often in the kennel, too.

She finally crept out of her small crate one morning. Eyeing me carefully, she waddled over to her bowl and poked her nose into it. There were a lot of different things in that bowl—some soft meat, pieces of broccoli, and chunks of apple. I didn't like the apples or the broccoli, and I didn't see what Stinkerbelle saw in them, but Casey seemed to enjoy them. He would sometimes take one and peck at it until it was gone.

I treated Stinkerbelle as I would a very scared kitten, and just let her become used to me being there. She seemed afraid of me, but was always very interested in Casey. And Casey was always interested in the skunk. Maybe they liked each other because they were each a deep, glossy black, with shiny black eyes.

Friends play with each other a lot, and different friends play different games. With other dogs I might play Get-the-Ball-First or Steal-the-Stick. Cats were pretty good at Chase Me. Sometimes we played Wrestling.

Casey and I played Sit-on-Lily's-Head a lot.

The skunk, though? I tried bringing a ball into the kennel with me, but she was unimpressed. I shook Craig's old socks, and she just stared at me, amazed. I tried to picture the skunk playing Sit-on-Lily's-Head, but it didn't seem likely.

It did seem that the more time I spent with

Stinkerbelle, the more comfortable she became. Eventually she forgot she was afraid and would sniff me all over, and sniff all over the kennel, and even went up to Casey to sniff.

Casey didn't sniff back. Crows just don't seem to be interested in that sort of thing.

Then Stinkerbelle curled up on her bed, so I curled up with her. I thought Maggie Rose should let Brewster in to sleep with us.

"I have good news," Dad said at breakfast one morning. I was crouched by Bryan's chair, because Bryan is the most likely to drop a piece of food on the floor. I like Bryan very much at mealtimes.

"You're going to let me have that electric skateboard?" Craig guessed.

"Of course not," Dad replied. Craig's legs kicked a little under the table.

"We're going to build a swimming pool?" Bryan suggested.

"A what?" Dad sputtered. Mom started laughing.

"Jason's parents are putting in a pool," Bryan pointed out.

"Everyone, stop talking," Dad said.

"Does it have to do with animals?" Maggie Rose asked. Bryan dropped a piece of toast and I pounced.

"Yes!"

"With the skunk?" my girl guessed.

"Right again, Maggie Rose!" Dad replied.

"We're getting an electric skateboard for the skunk?" Craig asked, sounding surprised.

Dad groaned.

"The skunk's getting a swimming pool?" Bryan demanded.

Now everyone was laughing.

"No. Thanks for the great ideas, but we're taking the skunk to the wildlife sanctuary," Dad went on. "Want to come, Maggie Rose? Lily too, of course. Your mom said Lily and the skunk have really bonded."

"They have," Mom affirmed.

Maggie Rose nodded. Then she looked around the table.

"Can Craig and Bryan come, too?" she asked.

Dad raised his eyebrows.

"Nice of you to think of the boys, Maggie Rose," he said. "Isn't it, you two? Do you guys want to come?"

"Sure," Craig said. "You did good helping to save it, Maggie Rose." Under the table, I saw his toe nudge Bryan's foot. "Hey Bryan, didn't Maggie Rose do a good job with the skunk?"

"Yeah," Bryan muttered.

"It was Lily who found the skunk," Maggie Rose said. "She's really the one who saved it."

A bit of scrambled egg slipped off Bryan's fork and hit the floor. I jumped on it. Mine!

After breakfast was over, we all went for a car ride. All meaning *all* of us! We climbed into the big car that can hold our whole family. Mom and Dad sat in the front. Craig and Bryan had the two middle seats. And Maggie Rose and I had the back seat to ourselves.

The first stop on the car ride was to Work. The whole family didn't often go to Work together. I pranced in with my tail wagging hard, excited to be with my family and my animal friends at the same time. Brewster, who always stays at Work, came stiffly out of his kennel with his tail wagging and sniffed at Craig and Bryan. Maggie Rose dropped down on her knees to give him a hug.

Casey croaked "Ree-ree," from the top of a stack of crates that held a mother cat and her three new kittens. The kittens were too young to come out and play yet, and the

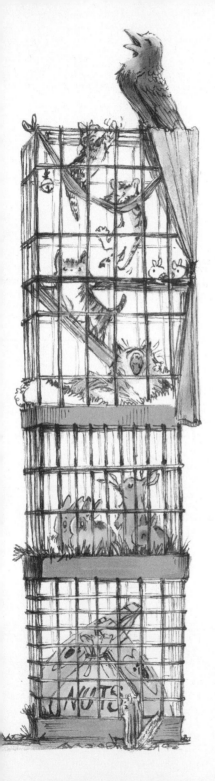

mother hissed at Casey, so Dad shooed him off the crates. Casey flew over Bryan's head (Bryan ducked) and perched on a bookshelf on the other side of the room.

Mom brought Stinkerbelle out in the crate. I went up and stuck my nose through the wire.

The skunk was huddled in a corner, and she seemed unhappy. But when she saw me, she jumped to her feet and waddled over to touch her nose to mine.

"Lily really is amazing," Mom said. "I'm glad she's here. This will

103

be much less stressful for the skunk with a friend nearby."

I heard wings overhead, and Casey swooped down to perch on the skunk's crate.

"Say goodbye to Stinkerbelle, Casey," Maggie Rose said.

Bryan snorted. "Stinkerbelle? Seriously?"

The skunk lifted her nose toward the roof of her crate. Casey lowered his beak and peered in at her.

"Look, they're really saying goodbye!" Maggie Rose exclaimed. Bryan rolled his eyes.

Dad picked up the skunk's crate and carried it to the car. He put it on the floor of the back seat where Maggie Rose and I were sitting. I could tell that the skunk was scared when the big car started to move, so I hopped down to be close to her.

I sat near the crate and leaned against the wire, so that the skunk could feel my fur. She leaned against me from the other side, and I knew that it made her feel safer.

Another car ride! I wondered where we were going now. Were we going to see more squirrels get sucked into a hose?

I hoped not. I didn't think my skunk friend would enjoy that at all.

12

When the car stopped moving, Maggie Rose put on my leash and took me out. We were in a parking lot with lots of cars and trucks, but the scents filling my nose were not metal and oil and gas. They were animals. Many animals, and they were very near.

Not dogs, though. I was the only dog.

There were squirrels, of course. (There seem to be squirrels everywhere.) And people.

I could definitely smell people. Deer, too—that was a smell I knew.

But the other smells—I couldn't identify them. I'd encountered some of them before, though. When Maggie Rose and Dad and I had been sleeping in the little cloth house, I'd smelled some of these odors in the woods. They'd been rubbed on the trees or were drifting on the air.

Animals. Big ones and little ones.

"Wait until you see this place," Dad said as we walked across the parking lot. "They have thousands of acres, and they have huge enclosures for all the animals they protect. They've got bears, lions, tigers. . . ."

"Tigers!" said Bryan. "I want to see the tigers."

"We will, after we drop off the skunk."

"Why do they have tigers, though?" asked Maggie Rose. "Did they bring them from India or China?"

"No, they're not a zoo. That's why I like this place so much," Dad explained. "They take in animals that can't live in the wild for some reason, or ones that have been kept as pets or in shows."

"Nobody should keep animals like that!" Maggie Rose said angrily.

"You're right," Dad agreed. "Nobody should keep wild animals as pets at all. Those animals can't always be released back into the wild—they never learned to hunt. So they come here."

"That's like Stinkerbelle," Maggie Rose said. "She can't live in the wild. . . ."

"So she can live here," Dad finished. He looked down at my skunk friend in her crate. "Welcome home, Stinkerbelle."

We walked in through a big gate, and Dad shook hands with a man who had hair underneath his nose and who smelled like coffee and ham and mustard. He lived with two different dogs. I could tell when I sniffed his shoes.

"Oh," said the man, looking down at me. "We don't usually allow dogs."

"Lily has a job to do," Maggie Rose said firmly. I wagged to hear my name, and wondered if we were going to play soon. "She helps Stinkerbelle stay calm."

The man looked surprised. Mom nodded. "My daughter's right."

"Fair enough." Nose-Hair Man led us along hard paths set into the dirt. There were fences on either side, and on either side of the wire were big stretches of grass.

Something was sleeping behind and alongside one of the fences, in a sunny spot. It looked like a huge pile of brown fur. Was it a dog? It was bigger than any dog I'd ever seen. And it didn't smell doglike.

It smelled . . . big. And male. And inter-esting! I pulled on the leash, trying to tug Maggie Rose toward the heap of fur.

"No, Lily—you can't sniff a bear!" she said, pulling me back.

I whined with frustration. The heap of fur made a snorting sound and rolled over, stretched four paws, and collapsed back into sleep again.

"That's Winston," said Nose-Hair Man. "He likes nothing better than a nap in a sunny spot. And here's the home we've made for your skunk!"

He stopped by a little house and pointed proudly.

The house had three wooden sides, and a fourth side

made of wire like the fences. The wire side had a small open door in it, and enclosing the entire house was a big dog kennel with a roof. But there wasn't a dog in it, and my nose told me there never had been. I would be the first!

"She'll be safe in here," the man said. "The wire roof will keep off any flying predators—there are hawks and owls around."

"Let's put her crate in and open it up," Mom suggested.

I watched alertly as Nose-Hair Man opened up the gate of the kennel, because my nose had picked up the scent of chicken treats, and I am very interested in chicken. Mom put Stinkerbelle's crate inside and slipped open its door. Then she came out, and the man shut and latched the kennel gate.

We watched. The skunk did not stir.

"She's scared," Maggie Rose said softly.

"She's right to be cautious in a new environment," said Dad.

"We haven't fed her yet this morning, so she'll probably come out to get some food," Mom told my girl.

"We put some berries and vegetables and a little bit of cooked chicken in her tray, inside the house," Nose-Hair Man said. My ears perked up when he said "chicken."

Mom nodded. "A nice balanced meal."

We watched some more. Nothing happened. I yawned, not understanding any of this.

"This is boring," Bryan complained. "Hey, look, goats! Can we pet them?"

Nose-Hair Man nodded. "That's the petting area."

"Go ahead. Craig, will you go with him?"

Mom said. "Maggie Rose, how about you? Don't you want to see the goats?"

My girl nodded. "But I want to make sure Stinkerbelle's okay first," she explained.

"That's my game warden girl," Dad said.

The boys left. I watched them go, and looked up at my girl to see what was happening now. Was I the only one who knew about the chicken?

It seemed that we were all still watching my skunk friend. But she wasn't doing much. Was she taking a nap inside her crate?

If we were supposed to play with the skunk, I would have to be let inside. And if that's what everyone wanted, maybe I'd get some chicken out of it.

I went to the kennel gate and pawed at it. I looked up at Maggie Rose.

13

Lily should go into the cage with Stinker-belle!" Maggie Rose exclaimed. I heard my name and figured she was talking about letting me play with my friend. I licked her knee to show her that I loved how she always understood what I needed.

"Well, I don't know. . . ." Nose-Hair Man replied doubtfully.

"They're friends," my girl told him.

"See, now that the skunk is here, the crit-ter's safety is my responsibility. If I put a dog in there and something happens, I get in a lot of trouble."

"Lily is something of an ambassador at our rescue," Mom explained. "She greets almost every animal who stays with us. It's amazing how she helps them calm down. She's been inside a kennel with the skunk every day. My daughter is right—Lily probably will help the skunk feel at home here."

"It's against the rules," the man said, his nose hair twitching.

I was getting impatient. I barked and Stinkerbelle reacted by sticking her face out of her crate and gazing at me. Nearly all animals wish they could bark like a dog.

"See? She wants Lily to help her feel better!"

"It doesn't look like the food is luring the skunk out, but she's okay with the dog," Dad observed reasonably.

"She gets hungry enough, she'll come out," Nose-Hair drawled.

"But that's not right," Maggie Rose argued. "Then she'll be scared *and* hungry."

The man scratched at the hair under his nose, and I found myself sitting and itching at my ear in response. "You do make yourself a good point there, young lady." He sighed. "Well, I guess it's worth a shot." The man unlatched the gate and I trotted inside.

I looked around with interest. There was
a hollow log along the back, and over in the
little house I could smell a bowl full of food—
the chicken!—and another with water.

I stuck my head into the crate. There was
Stinkerbelle, who had backed up and was
crouched low to the ground, not moving.

I wagged at her so that she'd know this
was a safe place to be. She lifted her head. I

wagged some more.

Then I turned around to check out the bowls in the little house.

After a moment, I heard a very soft rustling behind me. Stinkerbelle was following. When I stuck my head in the open doorway to the little house, she brushed right past me and put her nose next to mine in the food bowl.

"Well, I'll be," Nose-Hair Man said softly.

I made room for her. She took up a piece of apple and crunched it. She could have the apples. That was fine with me. I was more interested in the pieces of chicken. I snapped them up and then lapped at a drink.

"Dad, isn't the skunk going to be lonely without Lily?" Maggie Rose asked softly.

"I don't think so," Dad said. "Skunks are solitary animals. They live alone. Sometimes when it's very cold, they'll find a burrow with other skunks inside and huddle up, but that's pretty rare. Most of the time they're by themselves. It's natural for them."

The skunk ate a little more. Then she moved over to the water dish and drank, too.

She lifted up her head with water dripping off her muzzle. I licked it off for her. Outside of the cage, Nose-Hair Man whistled softly.

"So they're not like the prairie dogs," Maggie Rose said.

"That's right," Dad agreed. "A prairie dog wouldn't be happy all by itself. They need to be in a group."

"A coterie," Maggie Rose said.

"You got it. But skunks are different."

Then the skunk turned her back on me and went over to one end of the hollow log. She poked her nose inside it. Then, slowly, she climbed inside.

I peeked into the hole in the log. At first all I could see was the skunk's rump. But then there was a rustling noise and the skunk turned herself around. Her little black face with her shiny eyes peered out at me.

The skunk sniffed my nose. I pulled my head back out and looked at Maggie Rose. Stinkerbelle had decided to play Hide-in-a-Log, and I'd done Find-the-Skunk. But Stinkerbelle didn't want to come out or play anything else. She seemed content to curl up in her dark, quiet spot.

Now what?

There was much I did not understand. But I did see that I was in a dog kennel with a skunk, and that my girl and her family and a man with nose hair were all on the other side of the fence.

"Want to come out, Lily?" Maggie Rose asked softly.

Nose-Hair opened the gate, and I decided it was time for me to go back to my girl.

Stinkerbelle did not follow. When I went through the open gate, it was shut behind me. What were we doing? What about my skunk friend? Wasn't she coming back to Work with us?

Maggie Rose knelt and looked deeply into my eyes. "We have to go now, Lily. You did a good job taking care of Stinkerbelle the skunk, but this is where she lives now. We have to say goodbye."

I wagged. I didn't understand much, but I'd heard my friend's name, and I thought that the quiet, solemn way my girl was gazing at me delivered a clear message. When she patted her leg, I fell in step behind her. We were leaving Stinkerbelle behind.

"Craig! Bryan! Time to go!" Mom called.

When we reached the car and Maggie Rose slid into her seat, I hesitated, gazing back at the dog kennel. For just a moment, I thought I saw my friend's nose come out for one last look, but I could not be sure.

I jumped into my girl's lap and thought about all that had just happened. I was starting to understand that I would meet a lot of animals at Work. I would make friends with them and play with them. Some of them, like Casey, would stay. And some would go to new families or new places to live.

That was what the skunk was doing. The small house was her new place to live.

It was a good home. The skunk had food to eat and water to drink and a cozy place to nap. She didn't have anyone to play with, but she actually didn't really *like* playing with other animals, not even a dog—and there is no creature more fun to play with than a dog.

I would miss Stinkerbelle. But the skunk was in her new home, and I was with my girl.

We were both where we were supposed to be.

MORE ABOUT SKUNKS

Skunks are nocturnal. They are active at night and sleep during the day.

Skunks will eat almost anything, but their favorite food is insects and grubs. They will also eat small rodents, frogs, worms, birds' eggs, berries, mushrooms, bees, and wasps.

Skunks sometimes hunt venomous snakes. The venom does not hurt them.

Stinkerbelle is a striped skunk. The Latin name for this animal is *Mephitis mephitis*, which basically means "stinky stinky."

A group of skunks is called a surfeit.

Skunks usually make their dens in hollow logs or trees, brush piles, or inside the burrows of other animals. Sometimes they move in under porches or into abandoned buildings.

Skunks will spray only if they feel cornered or think that their babies are being threatened. You can usually stop a skunk from spraying by backing away and leaving it alone.

Skunks will warn before spraying by stamping their front feet, growling, spitting, and shaking their tails. The spotted skunk does a warning "dance" that looks like a handstand, in which it stands on its front feet and lifts its back legs into the air.

Skunks can spray up to ten or twelve feet. Their spray can be smelled a mile away.

If your pet gets sprayed by a skunk, keep it outside if possible. Don't wash your pet with tomato juice; that won't do anything to get rid of the smell. Pet stores sell special shampoos that can help get skunk spray out of fur. You can also use a mixture of hydro-gen peroxide and baking soda, maybe with a little dish soap added. Keep this mixture away from your pet's eyes and scrub and rinse as well as you can. The smell will fade in a few days.

READ ON FOR A SNEAK PEEK AT
LILY TO THE RESCUE:
DOG DOG GOOSE, COMING SOON
FROM STARSCAPE

I am a dog, and my name is Lily. I have a girl, and her name is Maggie Rose.

Today Maggie Rose put me on a leash. That meant I was going someplace exciting!

I trotted on my leash beside Maggie Rose. Craig walked with us. He is Maggie Rose's much older brother, and from where I stand, he looks very tall. Maggie Rose has another brother named Bryan, but he is not as tall, and he was not walking with us today.

My job when I am walking with Maggie

Rose is to look for things that she might not notice, such as a squirrel who needs to be chased, or bushes where dogs have lifted their legs.

"Know what kind of ice cream cone you want, Maggie Rose?" Craig asked while I was busy sniffing one of those bushes.

"Strawberry, because it's pink. Pink's my favorite color," Maggie replied.

"I thought you liked vanilla ice cream with sprinkles on it," Craig objected.

Maggie Rose frowned. "That was last year, when I was in second grade. I'm a third-grader now, so I like strawberry."

Craig nodded. "Makes sense."

A car drove past us on the street. A dog had his head out the window, and he barked at me. I knew what he was trying to tell me: "I'm in the car and you're not! I'm in the car and you're not!"

He kept barking until the car turned a

corner. Some dogs are like that. They start barking and then they just don't stop, even if they have forgotten why they were barking in the first place. I am a well-behaved dog, and I do not do such things.

We walked a little more, and then Craig went inside a building while I stayed outside with Maggie Rose. In a little while, Craig was back. He was carrying an ice cream cone in each hand, which I thought was a wonderful thing to do!

They sat at a table, and I did Sit. I am extremely good at Sit. I was sure that when Maggie Rose noticed what an incredible Sit I was doing, I would get some of that ice cream. Nothing else would even make sense.

But then a loud, deep voice startled us all. "Go away!" a man shouted.

We all jumped. I looked over my shoulder. There was a parking lot behind us, and a man was standing at the edge of it, looking angrily into a little stretch of trees and bushes. "Go away!" he shouted again.

"Whoa," Craig said. "It's Mr. Swanson! You know, he lives two houses down." He raised his voice a little. "What's going on, Mr. Swanson?"

Mr. Swanson turned around to look at us. He walked up to our table and pointed one thumb over his shoulder. "Hi, kids. See the fox?"

Craig shook his head. "What fox?" said Maggie Rose.

Mr. Swanson pointed into the trees. "There. Right there. See it?"

We all looked into the woods. I lifted my nose, and I caught a scent that was new to me. It was like a male dog, but different—wilder and more fierce. I pulled on my leash a little, so that Maggie Rose would let me go and meet this new animal. We could play together!

I am very good at playing with other animals. I often go to a place called Work and play with all the animals there. Work is where Mom spends most of her time helping animals. She calls Work "the rescue."

Maggie Rose twitched. "I see it! Lily, do you see it? See the fox?"

That was a new word to me—"fox." It must be the name of the animal.

The fox was crouched behind a bush, so I could only catch a glimpse of short fur and bright eyes and ears that stood up in stiff triangles. He stared at us hard.

"He's here for the eggs," Mr. Swanson said.

"What eggs?" Maggie Rose asked.

"Come on, I'll show you."

Mr. Swanson took us toward a big wooden box in the middle of the parking lot. It had some bushes and flowers growing inside it.

"A goose laid some eggs right in this planter," Mr. Swanson said. "But a couple of days ago, some men were here fixing potholes in the parking lot, and I guess the noise scared her. She flew away and never came back."

"Oh no," said Maggie Rose.

When we reached the wooden box, Maggie Rose looked into it. She gasped.

Craig peered over her shoulder. "Whoa, look at that!"

"Well, now," Mr. Swanson said. "That's remarkable!"

I put my front feet on the edge of the wooden box so that I could see inside. There was something moving in there!

Actually, there were a lot of somethings. They were small and fuzzy, like the kittens I play with at Work sometimes. But they also had beaks, like my friend Casey the crow. (Casey spent some time at Work because Mom needed to help his wing, so we got to know each other really well.) They huddled together in a group making tiny peeping noises. Broken eggshells were all around them.

"The eggs hatched!" exclaimed Maggie Rose. "They're so cute!"

"They're cute, all right," Craig said. He didn't sound as happy as Maggie Rose did. "But where's their mom?"

ABOUT THE AUTHOR

W. BRUCE CAMERON is the #1 *New York Times* bestselling author of *A Dog's Purpose, A Dog's Journey, A Dog's Way Home,* and *A Dog's Promise;* the young-reader novels *Bailey's Story, Bella's Story, Ellie's Story, Lily's Story, Max's Story, Molly's Story, Shelby's Story,* and *Toby's Story;* and the chapter book series Lily to the Rescue. He lives in California.

Don't miss these
LILY TO THE RESCUE
adventures from
bestselling author
W. BRUCE CAMERON

Meet Lily, a rescue dog who rescues
other animals! Charming illustrations
throughout each book bring Lily and her
rescue adventures to life.

BruceCameronKidsBooks.com

Interior art credit: Jennifer L. Meyer

Heartwarming Puppy Tales for Young Readers from
W. BRUCE CAMERON

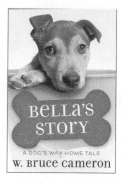

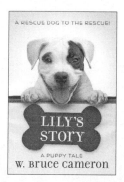

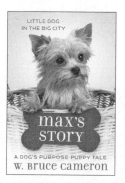

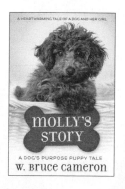

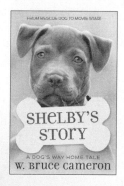

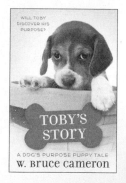

BruceCameronKidsBooks.com